This book belongs to:

_____

_____

Published by Poggle Press, an imprint of
Indigo Timmins Ltd • Pure Offices • Leamington Spa • Warwickshire CV34 6WE

ISBN: 978-0-9573501-1-3

www.springboardstories.co.uk

The Christmas Wish

Clare Bevan

Illustrated by
Simon Walmesley & James Walmesley

A Poggle Press publication

To Sian with love

The boy chose his favourite green
pen and wrote as neatly as he could:

Dear Father Christmas,

I would really like a friendly dragon,
but it might sizzle your sleigh.

So please can you send me enough
snow to build a Snow Dragon instead?

Thank you, love from....

Then he signed his name with a fancy squiggle
and opened his bedroom window.

'Winter wind, winter wind, set my wish free. Ask
Father Christmas to grant it for me,' he whispered.

And at once his letter whirled away
until it was just a dot in the grey sky.

A young crow, who was flying back to her tree, saw the fluttering paper and caught it in her beak.

'A moth,' she thought.

'How clever I am.'

'*How silly you are,*' cawed her mother. '*Anyone can tell this is a* magic spell. *I'll show it to the Snow Goose. He travels the world and sees many wonders, so perhaps he will know what to do.*'

When the crows spotted the Snow Goose flying by, they cackled noisily until he

SWOOPed down in a flurry of feathers.

They showed him the note and he peered at it for a long while.

'*I shall carry it to the Land of the Ice Giants,*' he honked at last.

'*They are fond of squiggles and will know what the spell means.*'

He gripped the note in his bill and away he soared.

Over the woods, over the towns,

over the empty beaches

and the stormy seas,

until he came to a wild place
where the rocks were shaped like
howling wolves.

The Snow Goose landed with a clatter. A dozing ice giant (who had been dreaming about warm slippers) woke with such a loud sneeze, he blew the bird into his breakfast bowl.

He lifted it out gently, gave it a shake, then wiped away the blobs of porridge with his huge hanky.

'What can I do for you, my little flappy friend?'

he boomed.

The letter was smudged and rather sticky, but the giant could still read most of the words.

'Ah,' he said sadly. '*I'm afraid I'm too clumsy to make snowflakes but I have an idea...*'

He fed the Snow Goose some ice-cold cake crumbs and tickled its head. Then he pulled a silver hair from his icy beard and used it to tie the note around the bird's long neck.

'*Take your message to the palace of the Frost Queen,*' he said. '*She is the artist who decorates our world with her sparkly paints, so perhaps she can weave snowflakes too.*'

The Snow Goose flew from rock to cloud, from cloud to mountain, and as he flew he chanted:

'Crow and goose and giant kind –
Now I have a queen to find.'

He followed a pathway of moonlight until he reached the glittering turret of a palace, and there was the Frost Queen leaning from her lofty window to paint the ivy leaves.

The queen laughed as the Snow Goose landed on a wobbly ledge. Then she reached out to unlace the boy's letter and she smiled at the green writing.

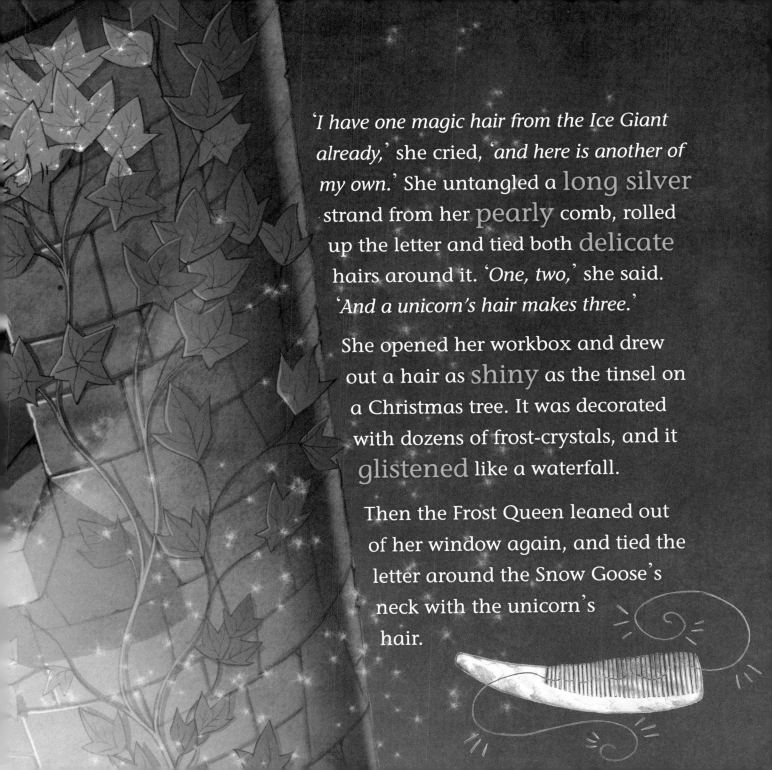

'*I have one magic hair from the Ice Giant already,*' she cried, '*and here is another of my own.*' She untangled a long silver strand from her pearly comb, rolled up the letter and tied both delicate hairs around it. '*One, two,*' she said. '*And a unicorn's hair makes three.*'

She opened her workbox and drew out a hair as shiny as the tinsel on a Christmas tree. It was decorated with dozens of frost-crystals, and it glistened like a waterfall.

Then the Frost Queen leaned out of her window again, and tied the letter around the Snow Goose's neck with the unicorn's hair.

'You must take your letter to the Wish-Wizard,' said the Frost Queen. 'But *fly swiftly*. It is already Christmas Eve and the morning will not wait.'

The Snow Goose searched the sky, and as he flew he chanted again:
'Crow and goose, giant and queen –
Where can a wizard's cave be seen?'

His wide wings drummed the air, and a lonely polar bear saw him skim past the moon like a shadow. 'There's magic in the air tonight,' it thought. 'I hope there's some for me.'

Beyond the moon, the Snow Goose could see the Sky Sisters counting stars. They swished their purple robes and peered at him through their telescopes.

'*What do you want?*' they called. '*And why are you here?*'

'*I need the Wish-Wizard,*' the weary Snow Goose honked politely. '*I seem to be lost.*'

'Water and ice,' laughed the sisters. '*That's our advice.*'

So the Snow Goose circled the ocean and the icebergs until he spotted a blue cavern. This was the Wish-Wizard's den, and few wanderers had ever found it. The old wizard was sitting in the cave-mouth, with his book of spells and his basket of twinkling strings.

'What do you bring me, Snow Goose?' he asked. 'A feather from a phoenix? A scale from a mermaid's tail?'

'Three silver hairs and one small wish,' spluttered the bird. 'Will that do?'

'Three is my favourite number,' said the old Wish-Wizard, reading the boy's letter. 'And this is a good wish. Well done, my friend. Now you can fly home and rest.'

The wizard gathered up the shimmering hairs. His fingers wove a winter charm, and when the pattern was complete, he added a single white goose feather, which had fallen into his basket.

He whispered a secret word and clapped his hands. '*Perfect*,' he sighed. '*A Christmas snowflake – and not a second too soon.*'

And at that exact moment, a scarlet sleigh dived down.

'*Ho, ho, ho!*' boomed the driver merrily.

'*Just what I needed.*'

He put the snowflake in his sack and sprang away
with his reindeer, to visit one last rooftop.

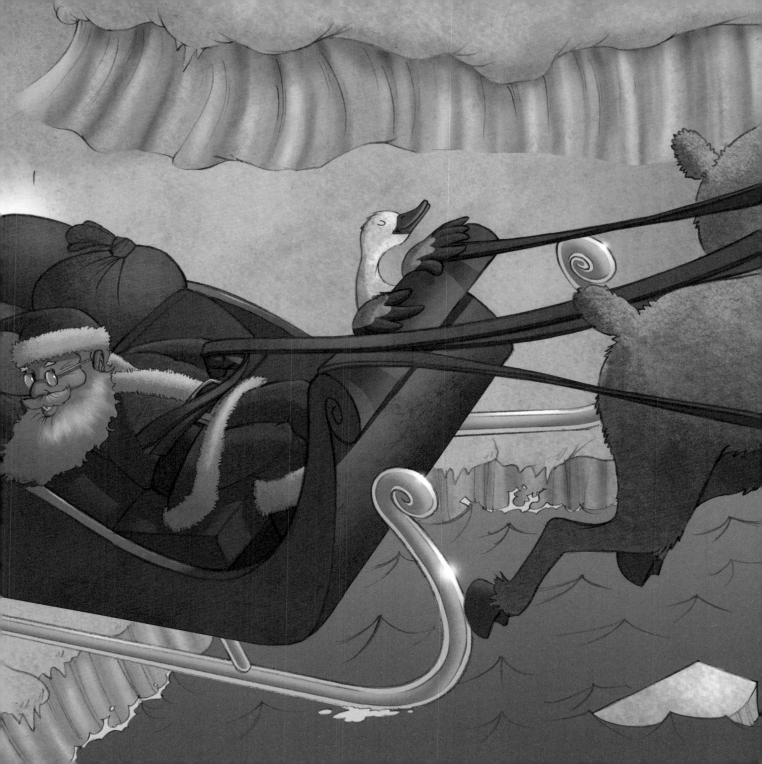

On Christmas morning the boy woke from a strange dream, full of wings and wishes and white feathers. His bedroom seemed strangely bright, and when he looked through his window, a sparkling snowflake fluttered past him to join all the others falling from the snowy sky.

At once, the boy pulled on his warm clothes and
wellingtons, then raced outside to build his
very own snow dragon, plus a whole crowd of
magical snow creatures to keep it company.

It was the best Christmas ever –
and the Snow Dragon thought so too!